The Five Mile Press
1 Centre Road, Scoresby
Victoria 3179 Australia
www.fivemile.com.au

Copyright © The Five Mile Press, 2012
All rights reserved

ISBN 978 1 74300 329 9

Printed in China 5 4 3 2 1

Ping Learns to Share

The Five Mile Press

Ping and his friends, Shi Shi and Yang, were very hungry. The pandas had run out of bamboo, their favourite food. They searched the forest high and low, tummies rumbling, but they couldn't find any more bamboo.

'What will we do?' cried Shi Shi.
'Let's look one more time,' said Yang. 'We'll go in
separate directions and meet back here later.'

All morning Ping trudged through the forest
until, tired and hungry, he headed home.
And that's when he found it ...
a huge patch of leafy bamboo!

Ping sat under a tree and happily
munched away, then he rubbed his
full tummy and sighed.
This will last me for days, he thought.
*But if I tell the others,
they will want to share it too.*

Later, as the sun was going down,
Ping and his friends shared their
last branch of bamboo. Ping took just a
small bite and left the rest for the others.
'Why are you eating so little, Ping?' asked Yang.
'Oh, I'm not that hungry tonight,' replied Ping,
thinking guiltily of his secret dinner.

That night, Ping couldn't sleep.
*I am being greedy keeping all that
bamboo for myself*, he thought.
Tomorrow I will share it with my friends.

But the next morning,
when Ping's tummy rumbled,
he crept quietly away and had a
breakfast feast, all by himself.

When they woke up, Ping's friends decided they
must leave home in search of food.
'I know where you can find lots of bamboo,'
squawked a pheasant, perched on a branch.
The bird pointed his wing towards a
mountain far far away.

When Ping told his friends that he was not
leaving with them, they were very sad.
'I am happy here and I don't
need much food,' lied Ping.

Yang and Shi Shi waved goodbye
and set off on their long journey.
'I hope you find lots of bamboo,' called Ping.
He knew he should have offered them
some bamboo for the trip,
but he didn't want to tell them
about his secret supply.

At first, Ping was quite happy. He had the
birds and the butterflies to keep him company,
and there was plenty to eat.
But the patch of bamboo grew smaller and smaller,
until one day there was nothing left. Ping rubbed his
rumbling tummy and thought about his friends
in their new home.

One afternoon, as Ping searched for tiny
scraps of food, the pheasant swooped down.
'Your friends found lots of bamboo and cosy
new homes,' chirped the bird.
Ping felt even more lonely and hungry.
'If only I had shared my bamboo,' he whimpered.

Ping remembered how much fun he used
to have playing with Shi Shi and Yang.
He missed their games of hide-and-seek.

Big tears began to roll down his face as
he realised how badly he had treated his friends.
He was soon sobbing so loudly
that he did not hear two familiar voices
calling out, 'Hello, Ping!'

'Don't cry, Ping,' said Shi Shi and Yang,
gathering around him. 'We've come back to
share the bamboo that we found.'
Wiping away his tears, Ping jumped to
his feet and hugged his friends.

'I've missed you two so much!' he cried.
'And I've been so greedy!'
Then Ping told his friends all about
the bamboo he had kept to himself.

'How could you just let us go hungry?'
demanded Yang angrily.
'You've been very selfish,'
said Shi Shi, shaking her head.

'I am so sorry,' wailed Ping.
'Will you please forgive me?'
He looked very sad and sorry.

Realising that Ping had truly learned
his lesson, his friends forgave him.
'From now on, we'll always stick together,' said Yang.
'From now on, I'll always share with
my friends,' promised Ping.
Munching their bamboo happily, the
three pandas watched the sunset together.